A Note to Parents and Teachers

Kids can imagine, kids can laugh and kids can learn to read with this exciting new series of first readers. Each book in the Kids Can Read series has been especially written, illustrated and designed for beginning readers. Humorous, easy-to-read stories, appealing characters, and engaging illustrations make for books that kids will want to read over and over again.

To make selecting a book easy for kids, parents and teachers, the Kids Can Read series offers three levels based on different reading abilities:

Level 1: Kids Can Start to Read

Short stories, simple sentences, easy vocabulary, lots of repetition and visual clues for kids just beginning to read.

Level 2: Kids Can Read with Help

Longer stories, varied sentences, increased vocabulary, some repetition and visual clues for kids who have some reading skills, but may need a little help.

Level 3: Kids Can Read Alone

Longer, more complex stories and sentences, more challenging vocabulary, language play, minimal repetition and visual clues for kids who are reading by themselves.

With the Kids Can Read series, kids can enter a new and exciting world of reading!

A Friend for Sam

Written by Mary Labatt

Illustrated by Marisol Sarrazin

Kids Can Press

Kids Can Read is a trademark of Kids Can Press

Kids Can Press acknowledges the financial support of the Ontario Arts Council, the Canada Council for the Arts and the Government of Canada, through the BPIDP, for our publishing activity.

Published in Canada by
Kids Can Press Ltd.
29 Birch Avenue
Toronto, ON M4V 1E2

Published in the U.S. by
Kids Can Press Ltd.
2250 Military Road
Tonawanda, NY 14150

www.kidscanpress.com

Edited by David MacDonald
Designed by Stacie Bowes and Marie Bartholomew
Printed in Hong Kong, China, by Wing King Tong Company Limited

The hardcover edition of this book is smyth sewn casebound.
The paperback edition of this book is limp sewn with a drawn-on cover.

CM 03 0 9 8 7 6 5 4 3 2 1
CM PA 03 0 9 8 7 6 5 4 3 2 1

National Library of Canada Cataloguing in Publication Data

Labatt, Mary, date.
    A friend for Sam / written by Mary Labatt ; illustrated by Marisol Sarrazin.

(Kids Can read)
ISBN 1-55337-374-X (bound).   ISBN 1-55337-375-8 (pbk.)

I. Sarrazin, Marisol, 1965– II. Title. III. Series: Kids Can read (Toronto, Ont.)

Kids Can Press is a l'(O)rUs™ Entertainment company

Joan looked out the window.

"It is a sunny day," she said.

"You can play outside, Sam."

Joan opened the door

and Sam went out.

"Have fun, Sam!" said Joan.

Sam looked at the backyard.

"This is not fun," she thought.

"I need a friend."

A robin hopped past.

"Good!" thought Sam.

"This robin can be my friend."

Sam ran after the robin.

"Woof," she said.

But the robin hopped away.

The robin flew

over the fence.

Then it was gone.

A frog hopped past.

"Good," thought Sam.

"This frog can be my friend."

Sam ran after the frog.

"Woof," she said.

But the frog hopped away.

The frog hopped

under the fence.

Then it was gone.

Sam looked at the fence.

"I need to get out," she thought.

"I need to find a friend."

Sam started to dig.

She dug and dug.

Dirt flew all around.

"Here I go," she thought.

Sam squeezed and squeezed.

At last she was out!

Sam went past garbage cans

and bicycles.

"Where can I find a friend?" she thought.

A black cat ran by.

"Woof," said Sam.

When the cat saw Sam,

it ran up a tree.

"Hiss," said the cat.

"A cat is not

a good friend for me," thought Sam.

A red squirrel ran by.

"Woof," said Sam.

When the squirrel saw Sam,

it ran up a tree.

"Chitter, chitter," said the squirrel.

"A squirrel is not

a good friend for me," thought Sam.

A green snake slid by.

"Woof," said Sam.

When the snake saw Sam,

it slid behind a rock.

"Ss-s-s," said the snake.

"A snake is not

a good friend for me," thought Sam.

"Hi puppy," said someone.

Sam looked around.

"Who is that?" she thought.

Two eyes looked through a fence.

Sam looked at the eyes.

The eyes looked at Sam.

Sam peeked through the fence.

She saw a little boy.

He was eating ice cream.

"I like you, puppy," said the boy.

He stuck the ice cream out for Sam.

Sam licked and licked.

"Yum!" she thought.

"Woof!" said Sam.

She jumped at the fence
and wagged her little tail.

The boy dropped the ice cream.

"You can have it, puppy," he said.

"Woof! Woof!" said Sam.

Sam gobbled the ice cream.

"Yum! Yum!" she thought.

"I like this boy!

He can be my friend!"

"I have to go in now, puppy,"

said the little boy.

"Woof!" said Sam

and she started for home.

Sam went past the cat,

past the squirrel

and past the snake.

She went past the garbage cans

and the bicycles.

Then she squeezed into her own backyard.